MOON GIRL AND DEVIL DINOSAUR

LUNELLA LAFAYETTE is teased by other kids, who call her **MOON GIRL** and laugh at her inventions. Who needs friends when you have gizmos and books? She's just biding her time until she can get into a **REAL** school for genius kids like her.

There's only one problem: Lunella has the **INHUMAN** gene, which means she could transform into a freak with powers at any moment! She found a device that could help stop it – the **OMNI-WAVE PROJECTOR**.

When activated, it created a **TIME PORTAL** that brought forth angry cavemen called **KILLER FOLK** and a **BIG, RED DINOSAUR!** The Killer Folk stole the projector and fled, leaving Lunella eager to retrieve it!

While hiding the dinosaur in her secret lab at school, a fire broke out. Devil Dinosaur and Lunella helped rescue everyone inside, but another hero has finally found them: **THE HULK**. Despite their heroism, he has demanded Devil Dinosaur leave with him…

BFF #4:
Hulk + Devil Dinosaur = 'Nuff Said

Writers: Brandon Montclare & Amy Reeder
Artist: Natacha Bustos
Colorist: Tamra Bonvillain
Letterer: VC's Travis Lanham
Production Design: Manny Mederos
Editors: Mark Paniccia & Emily Shaw
Cover: Amy Reeder

DEVIL DINOSAUR CREATED BY JACK KIRBY

Special Thanks to Sana Amanat and David Gabriel
Axel Alonso **Editor in Chief**   Joe Quesada **Chief Creative Officer**
Dan Buckley **Publisher**   Alan Fine **Executive Producer**

ABDOPUBLISHING.COM

Reinforced library bound edition published in 2018 by Spotlight,
a division of ABDO, PO Box 398166, Minneapolis, Minnesota 55439.
Spotlight produces high-quality reinforced library bound editions for
schools and libraries. Published by agreement with Marvel Characters, Inc.

Printed in the United States of America, North Mankato, Minnesota.
042017
092017

THIS BOOK CONTAINS
RECYCLED MATERIALS

marvelkids.com
© 2017 MARVEL

PUBLISHER'S CATALOGING IN PUBLICATION DATA

Names: Reeder, Amy ; Montclare, Brandon, authors. | Bustos, Natacha ; Bonvillain,
Tamra, illustrators.
Title: Hulk + Devil Dinosaur = 'nuff said / writers: Amy Reeder ; Brandon
Montclare ; art: Natacha Bustos ; Tamra Bonvillain.
Description: Reinforced library bound edition. | Minneapolis, Minnesota : Spotlight,
2018. | Series: Moon Girl and Devil Dinosaur ; BFF #4
Summary: When the Hulk shows up at school demanding to take Devil Dinosaur
into protective custody, Lunella takes charge to defend her friend.
Identifiers: LCCN 2016961927 | ISBN 9781532140112 (lib. bdg.)
Subjects: LCSH: Schools--Juvenile fiction. | Adventure and adventurers--Juvenile
fiction. | Comic Books, strips, etc.--Juvenile fiction. | Graphic novels--Juvenile
fiction.
Classification: DDC 741.5--dc23
LC record available at https://lccn.loc.gov/2016961927

Spotlight

A Division of ABDO
abdopublishing.com

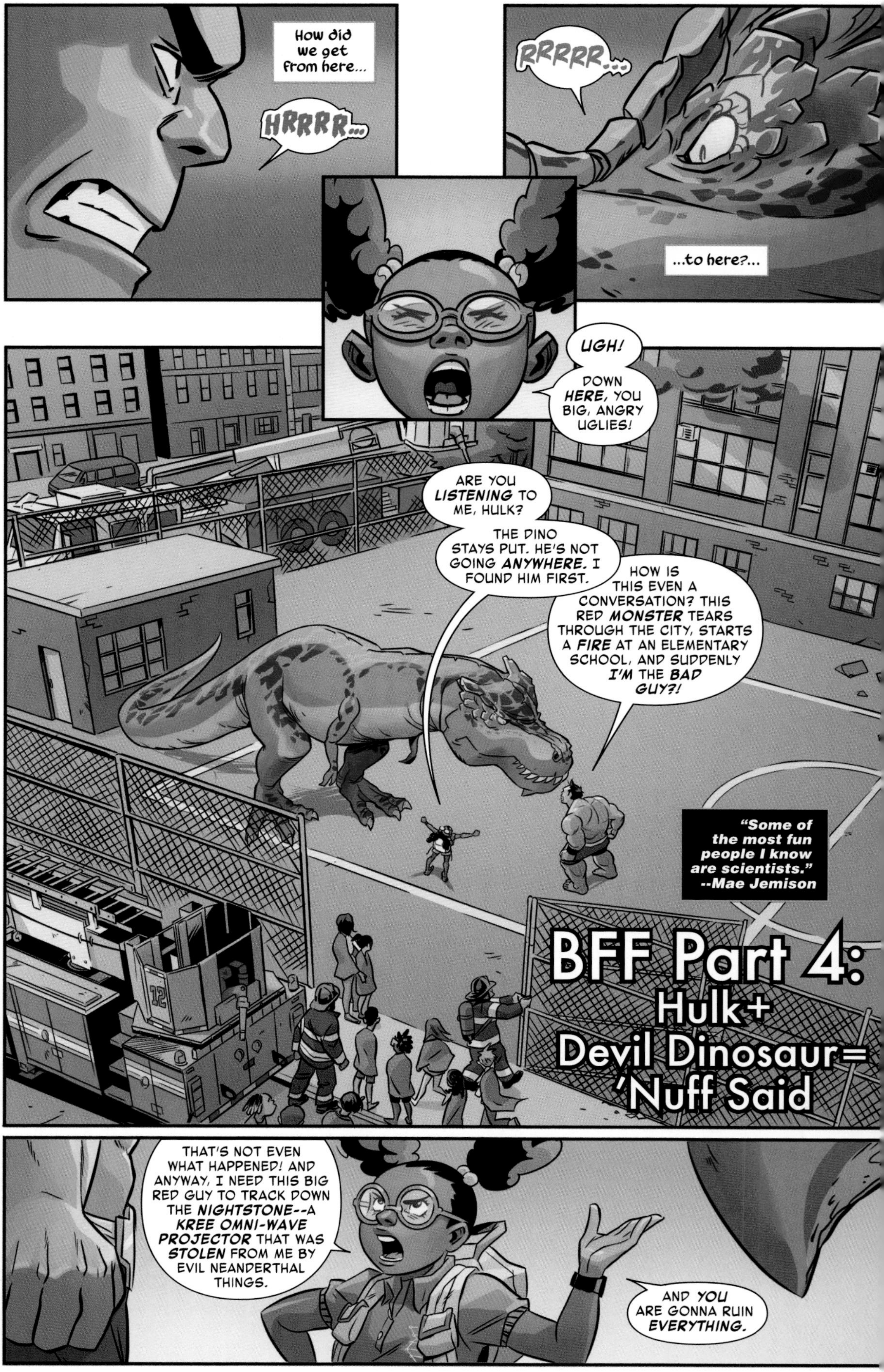

How did we get from here...
HRRRR...
RRRRR...
...to here?...
UGH!
DOWN HERE, YOU BIG, ANGRY UGLIES!
ARE YOU LISTENING TO ME, HULK?
THE DINO STAYS PUT. HE'S NOT GOING ANYWHERE. I FOUND HIM FIRST.
HOW IS THIS EVEN A CONVERSATION? THIS RED MONSTER TEARS THROUGH THE CITY, STARTS A FIRE AT AN ELEMENTARY SCHOOL, AND SUDDENLY I'M THE BAD GUY?!
"Some of the most fun people I know are scientists." --Mae Jemison
BFF Part 4:
Hulk+ Devil Dinosaur= 'Nuff Said
12
THAT'S NOT EVEN WHAT HAPPENED! AND ANYWAY, I NEED THIS BIG RED GUY TO TRACK DOWN THE NIGHTSTONE--A KREE OMNI-WAVE PROJECTOR THAT WAS STOLEN FROM ME BY EVIL NEANDERTHAL THINGS.
AND YOU ARE GONNA RUIN EVERYTHING.

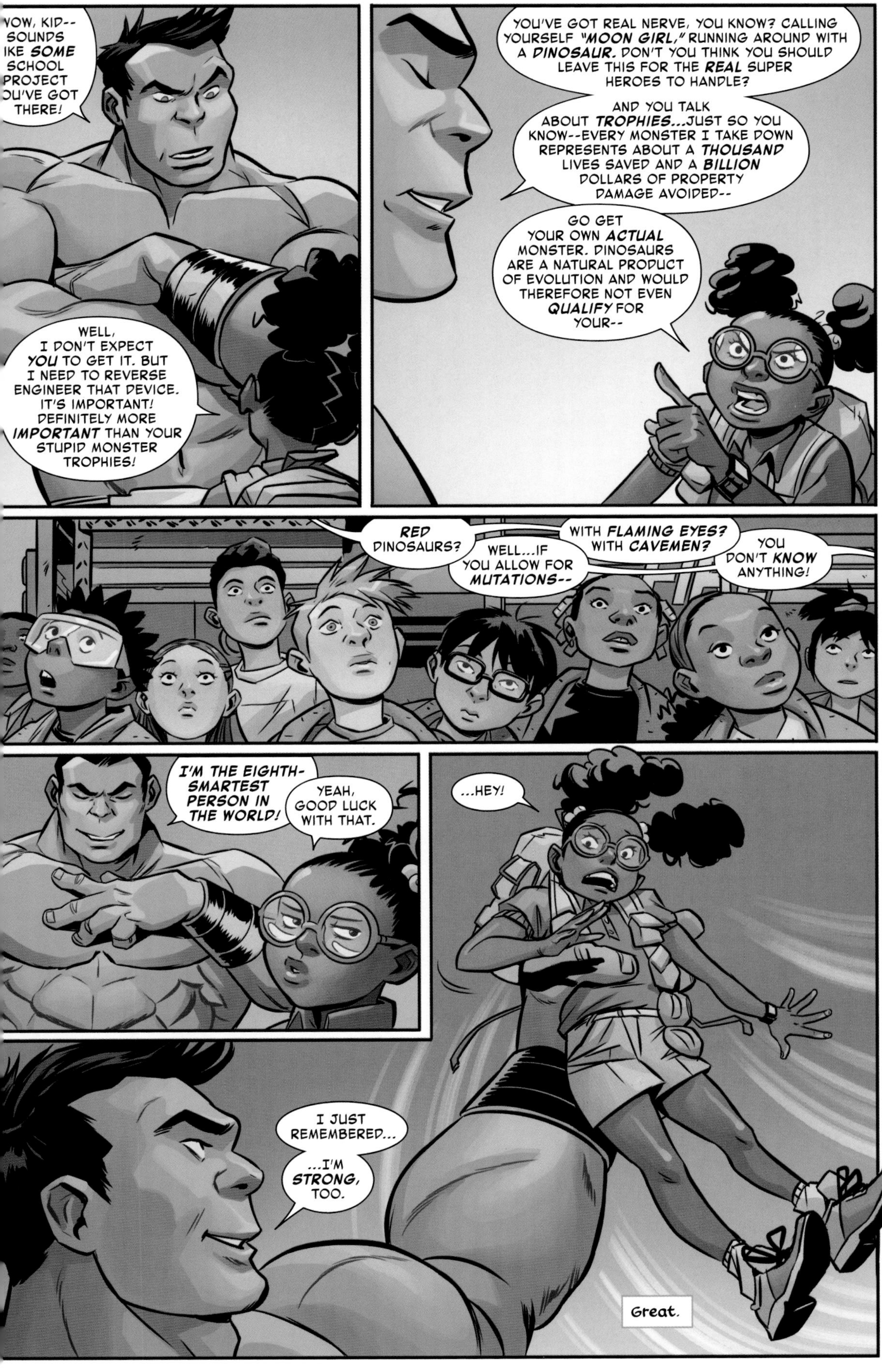
WOW, KID--SOUNDS LIKE SOME SCHOOL PROJECT YOU'VE GOT THERE!
WELL, I DON'T EXPECT YOU TO GET IT. BUT I NEED TO REVERSE ENGINEER THAT DEVICE. IT'S IMPORTANT! DEFINITELY MORE IMPORTANT THAN YOUR STUPID MONSTER TROPHIES!
YOU'VE GOT REAL NERVE, YOU KNOW? CALLING YOURSELF "MOON GIRL," RUNNING AROUND WITH A DINOSAUR. DON'T YOU THINK YOU SHOULD LEAVE THIS FOR THE REAL SUPER HEROES TO HANDLE?
AND YOU TALK ABOUT TROPHIES...JUST SO YOU KNOW--EVERY MONSTER I TAKE DOWN REPRESENTS ABOUT A THOUSAND LIVES SAVED AND A BILLION DOLLARS OF PROPERTY DAMAGE AVOIDED--
GO GET YOUR OWN ACTUAL MONSTER. DINOSAURS ARE A NATURAL PRODUCT OF EVOLUTION AND WOULD THEREFORE NOT EVEN QUALIFY FOR YOUR--
RED DINOSAURS?
WELL...IF YOU ALLOW FOR MUTATIONS--
WITH FLAMING EYES? WITH CAVEMEN?
YOU DON'T KNOW ANYTHING!
I'M THE EIGHTH-SMARTEST PERSON IN THE WORLD!
YEAH, GOOD LUCK WITH THAT.
...HEY!
I JUST REMEMBERED...
...I'M STRONG, TOO.
Great.

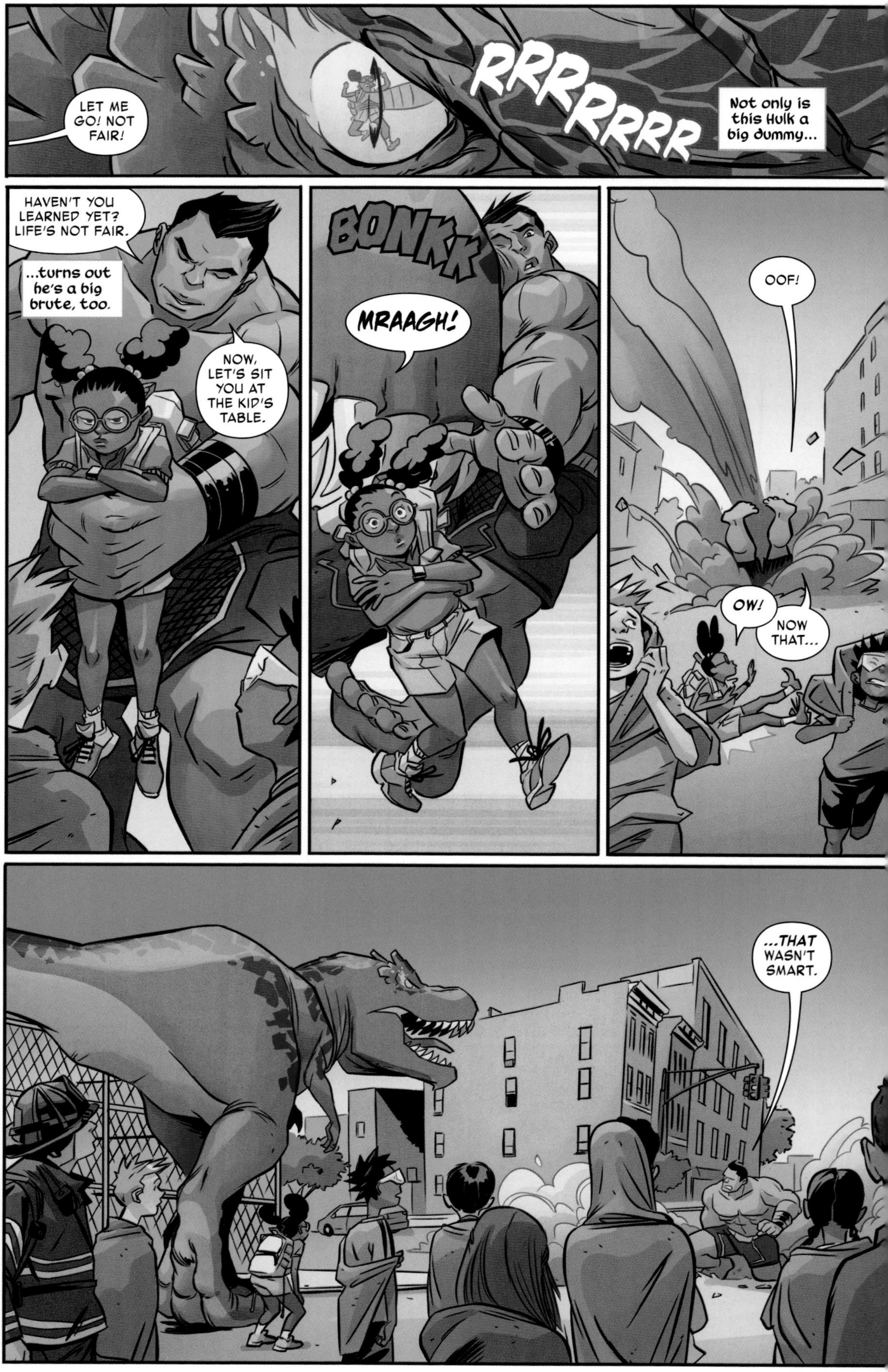
LET ME GO! NOT FAIR!
RRRRRRR
Not only is this Hulk a big dummy...
HAVEN'T YOU LEARNED YET? LIFE'S NOT FAIR.
...turns out he's a big brute, too.
NOW, LET'S SIT YOU AT THE KID'S TABLE.
BONKK
MRAAGH!
OOF!
OW!
NOW THAT...
...THAT WASN'T SMART.

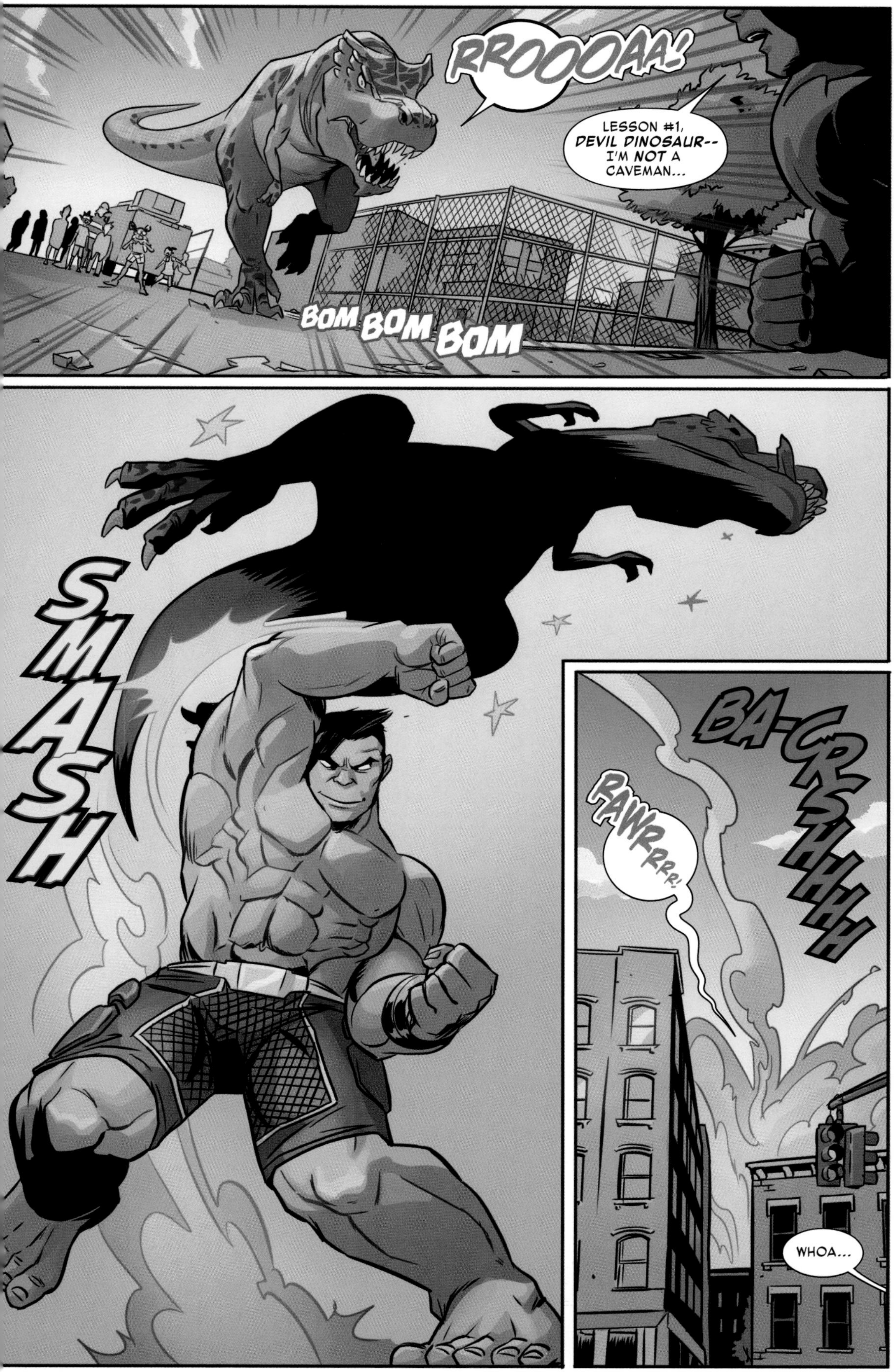
RROOOOAA!
LESSON #1, DEVIL DINOSAUR-- I'M NOT A CAVEMAN...
BOM BOM BOM
SMASH
BA-CRSHHHHH
RAWRRRR!
WHOA...

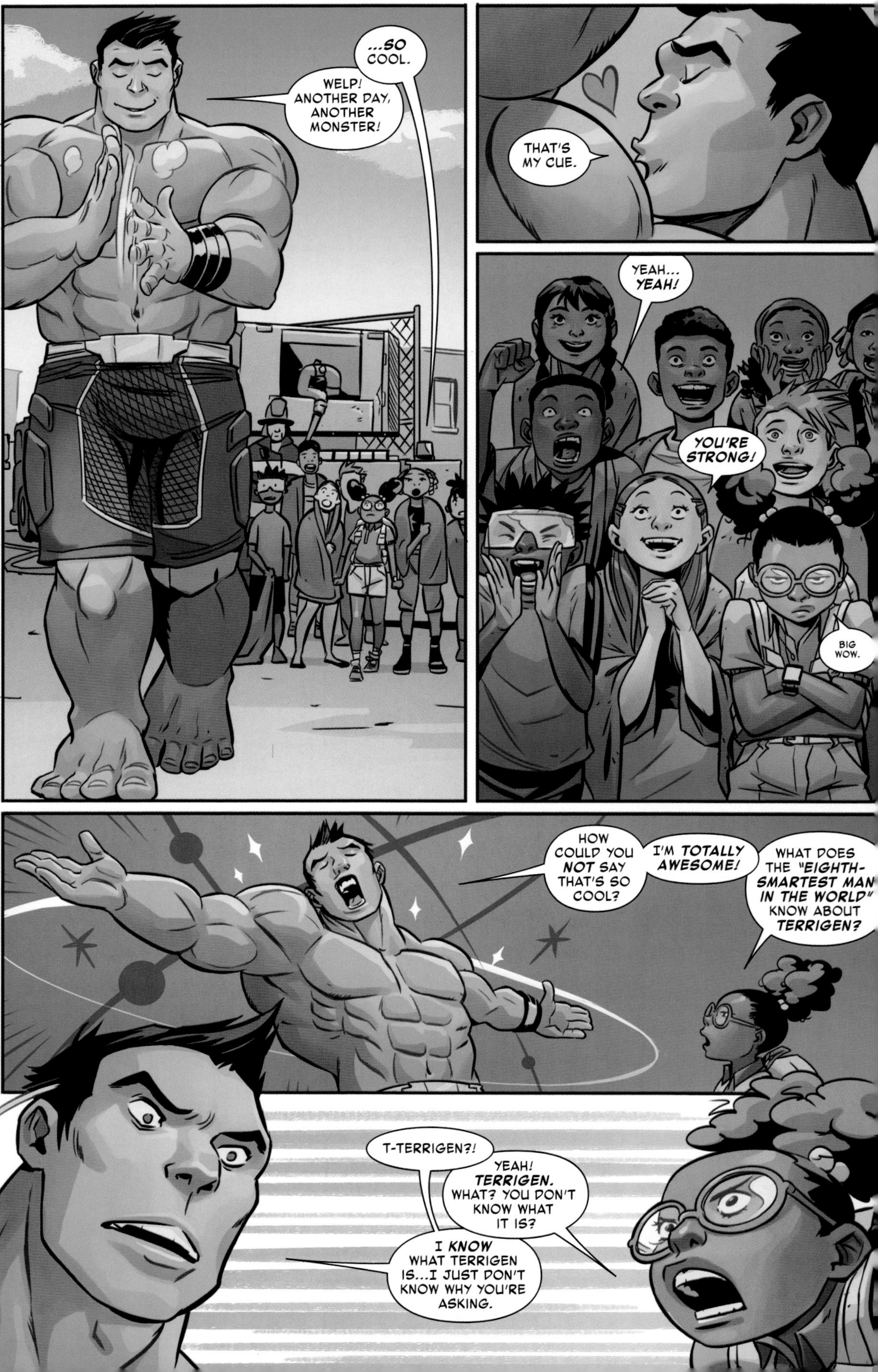
WELP! ANOTHER DAY, ANOTHER MONSTER!
...SO COOL.
THAT'S MY CUE.
YEAH... YEAH!
YOU'RE STRONG!
BIG WOW.
HOW COULD YOU NOT SAY THAT'S SO COOL?
I'M TOTALLY AWESOME!
WHAT DOES THE "EIGHTH-SMARTEST MAN IN THE WORLD" KNOW ABOUT TERRIGEN?
T-TERRIGEN?!
YEAH! TERRIGEN. WHAT? YOU DON'T KNOW WHAT IT IS?
I KNOW WHAT TERRIGEN IS...I JUST DON'T KNOW WHY YOU'RE ASKING.

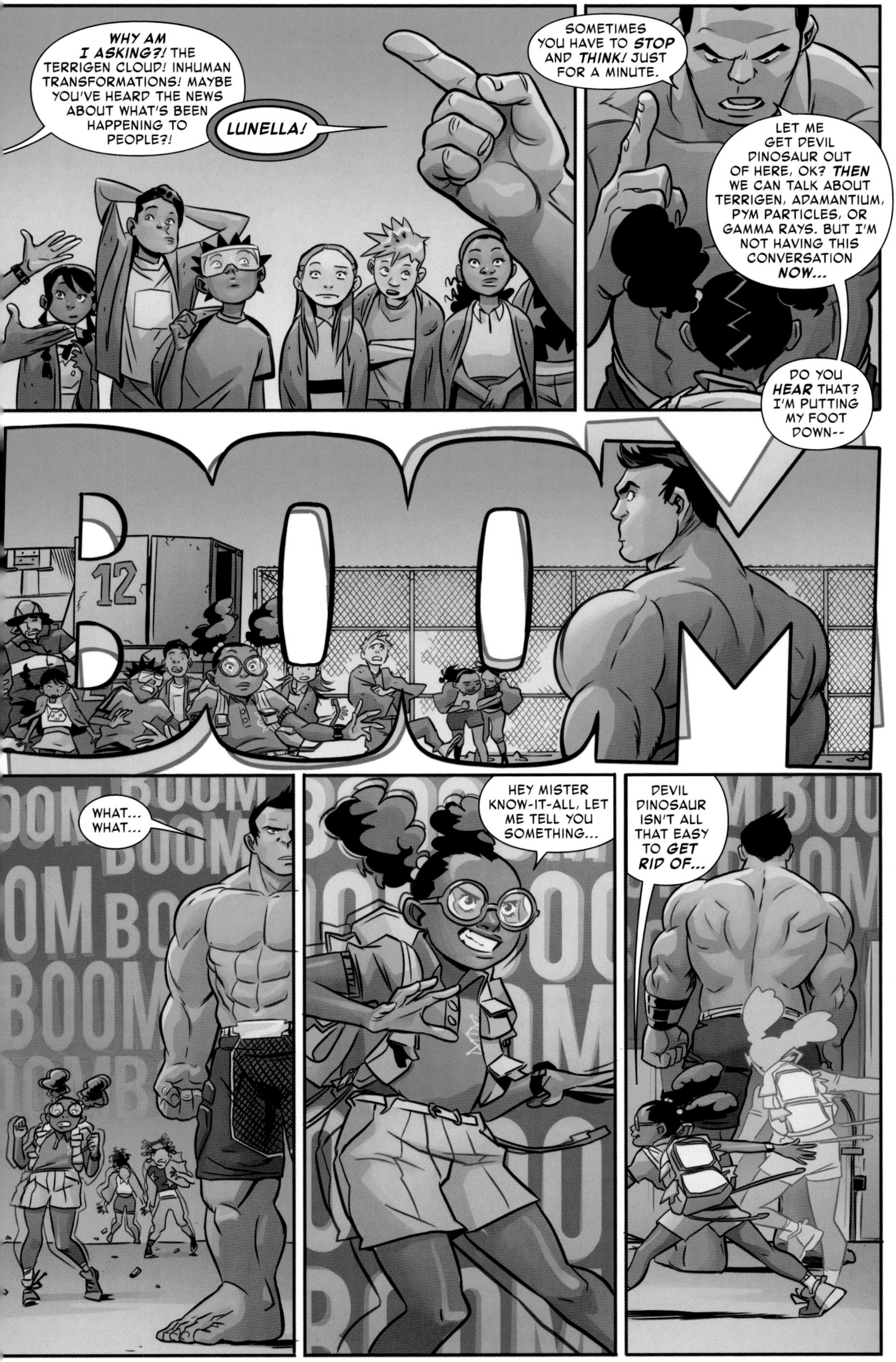
WHY AM I ASKING?! THE TERRIGEN CLOUD! INHUMAN TRANSFORMATIONS! MAYBE YOU'VE HEARD THE NEWS ABOUT WHAT'S BEEN HAPPENING TO PEOPLE?!
LUNELLA!
SOMETIMES YOU HAVE TO STOP AND THINK! JUST FOR A MINUTE.
LET ME GET DEVIL DINOSAUR OUT OF HERE, OK? THEN WE CAN TALK ABOUT TERRIGEN, ADAMANTIUM, PYM PARTICLES, OR GAMMA RAYS. BUT I'M NOT HAVING THIS CONVERSATION NOW...
DO YOU HEAR THAT? I'M PUTTING MY FOOT DOWN--
BOOM
12
WHAT... WHAT...
HEY MISTER KNOW-IT-ALL, LET ME TELL YOU SOMETHING...
DEVIL DINOSAUR ISN'T ALL THAT EASY TO GET RID OF...

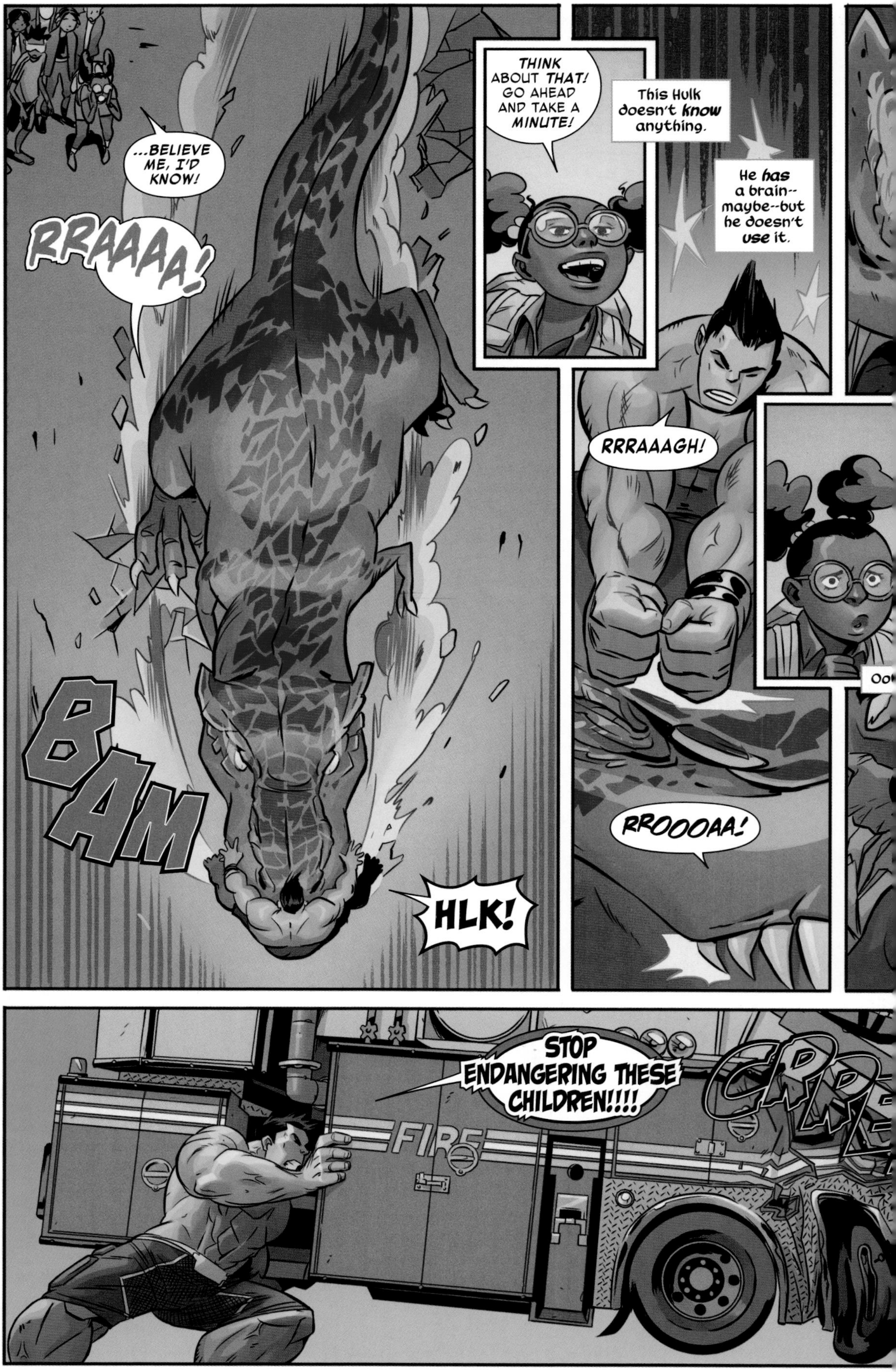

...BELIEVE ME, I'D KNOW!
RRAAAAA!
BAM
HLK!
THINK ABOUT THAT! GO AHEAD AND TAKE A MINUTE!
This Hulk doesn't know anything.
He has a brain--maybe--but he doesn't use it.
RRRAAAGH!
RROOOAA!
STOP ENDANGERING THESE CHILDREN!!!!
FIRE

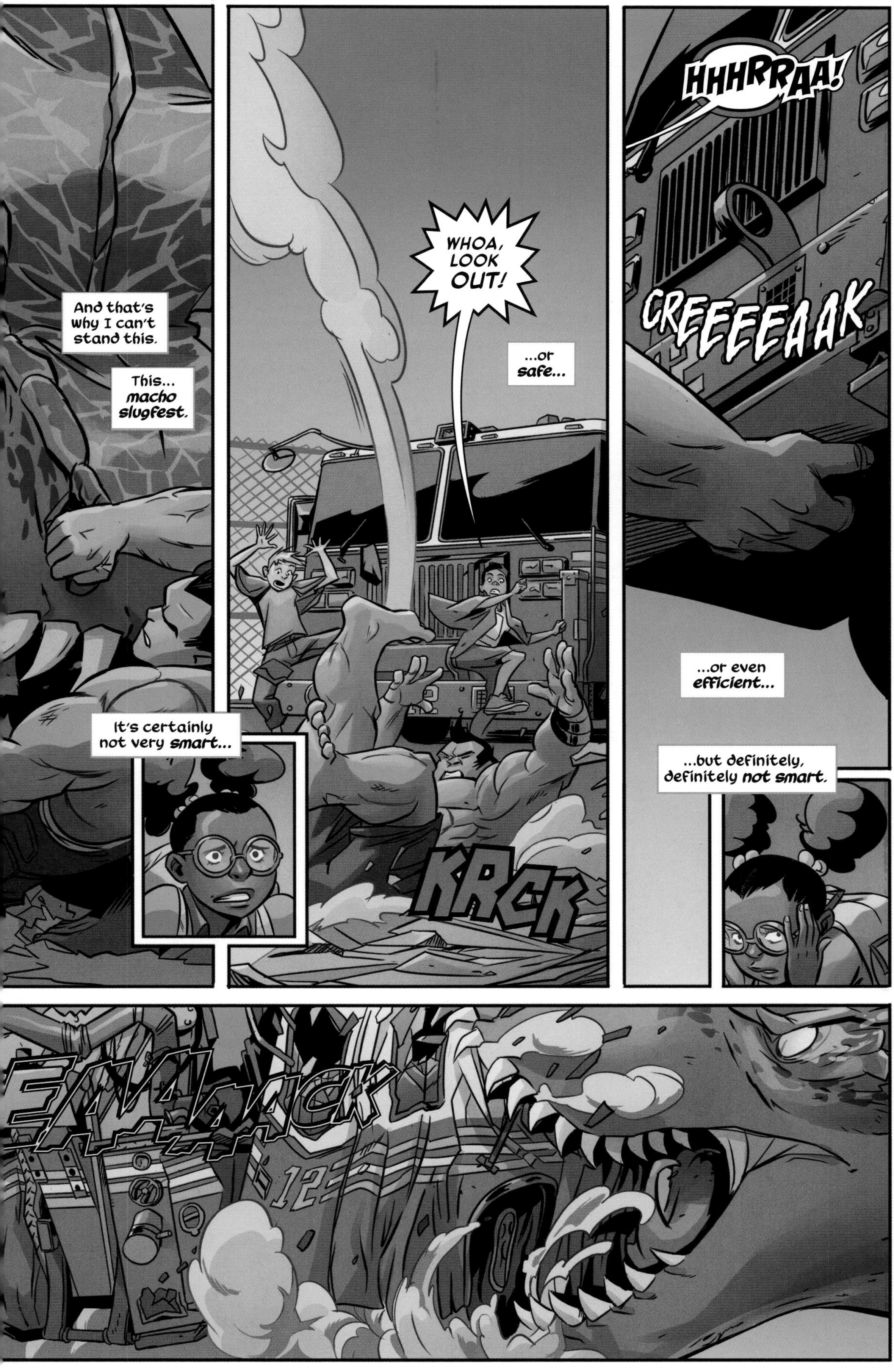

And that's why I can't stand this.
This... macho slugfest.
It's certainly not very smart...
WHOA, LOOK OUT!
...or safe...
KRCK
HHHRRAA!
CREEEEAAK
...or even efficient...
...but definitely, definitely not smart.

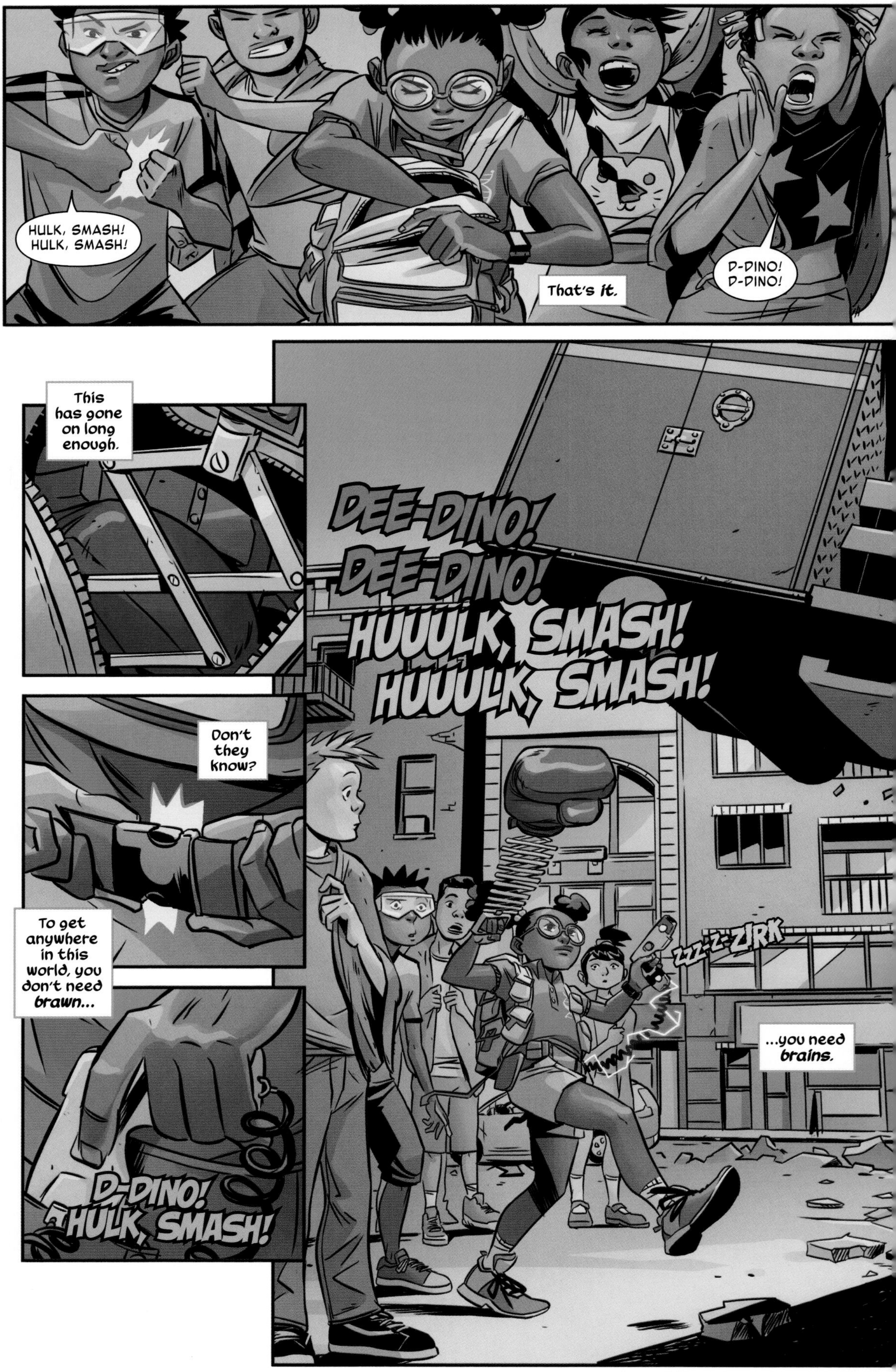
HULK, SMASH!
HULK, SMASH!
That's it.
D-DINO!
D-DINO!
This has gone on long enough.
Don't they know?
To get anywhere in this world, you don't need brawn...
D-DINO!
HULK, SMASH!
DEE-DINO!
DEE-DINO!
HUUULK, SMASH!
HUUULK, SMASH!
ZZZ-Z-ZIRK
...you need brains.

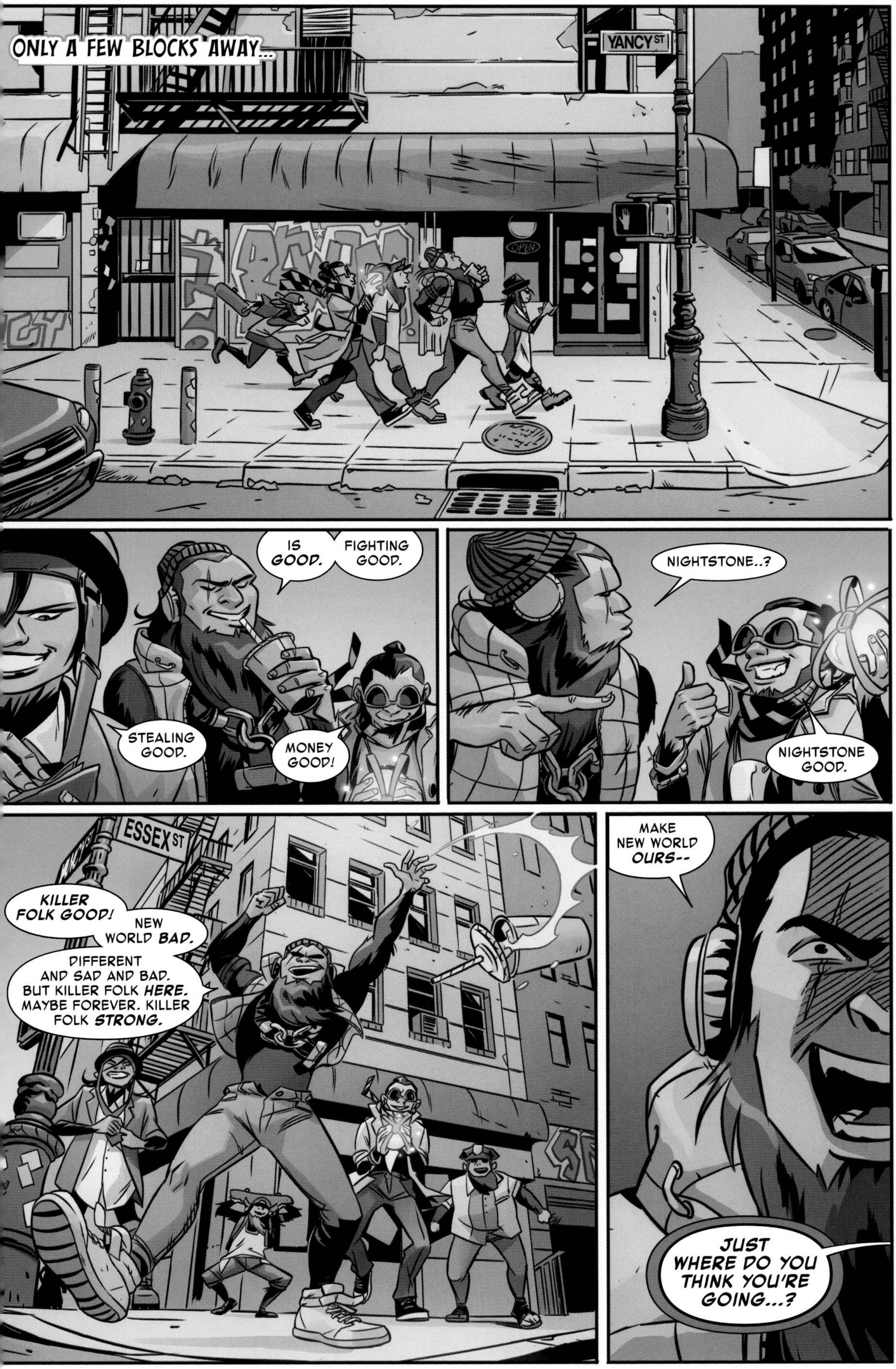

ONLY A FEW BLOCKS AWAY...
YANCY ST
OPEN
IS GOOD.
FIGHTING GOOD.
STEALING GOOD.
MONEY GOOD!
NIGHTSTONE..?
NIGHTSTONE GOOD.
ESSEX ST
KILLER FOLK GOOD!
NEW WORLD BAD.
DIFFERENT AND SAD AND BAD. BUT KILLER FOLK HERE. MAYBE FOREVER. KILLER FOLK STRONG.
MAKE NEW WORLD OURS--
JUST WHERE DO YOU THINK YOU'RE GOING...?

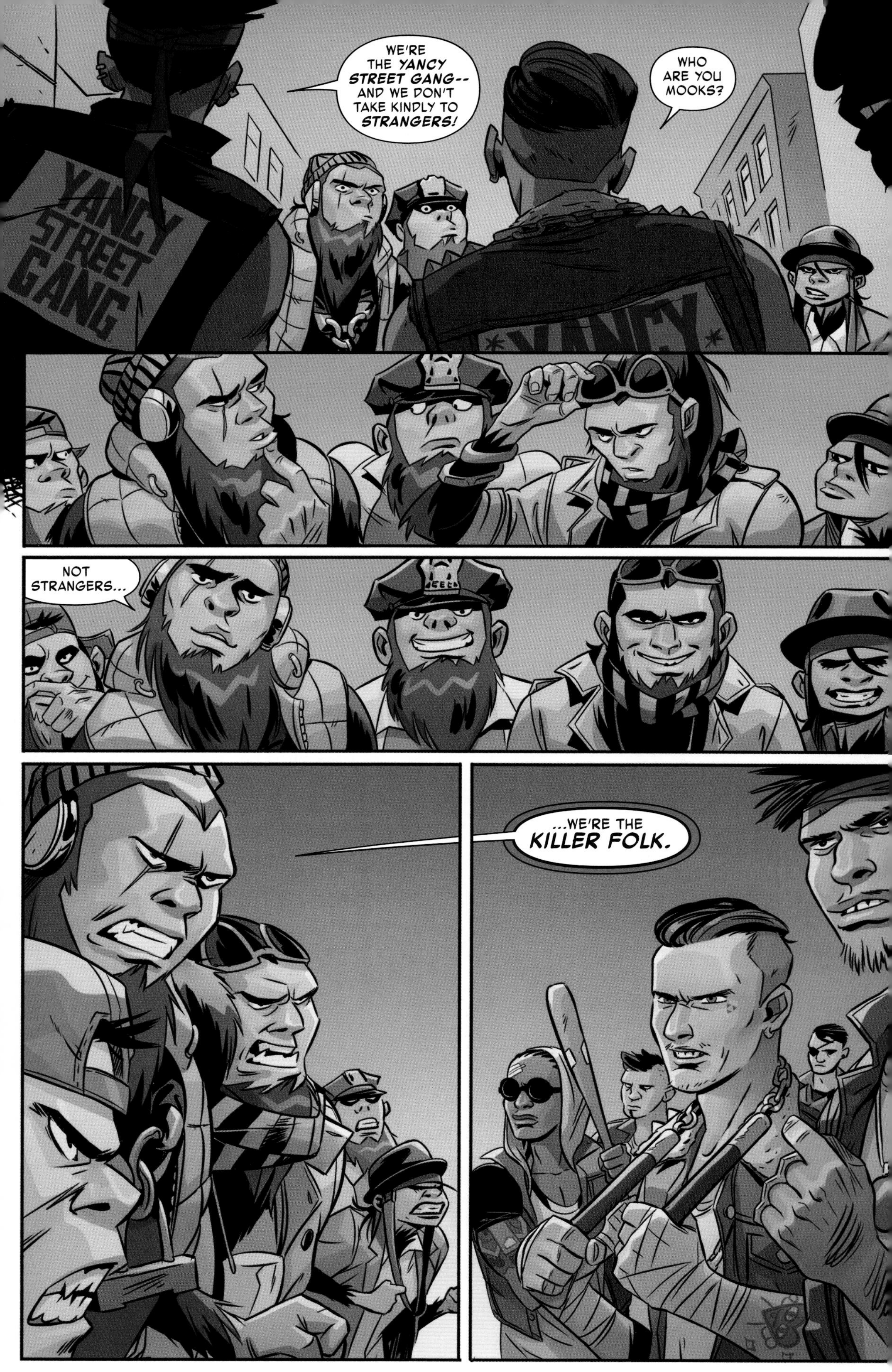
WE'RE THE YANCY STREET GANG-- AND WE DON'T TAKE KINDLY TO STRANGERS!
WHO ARE YOU MOOKS?
YANCY STREET GANG
NOT STRANGERS...
...WE'RE THE KILLER FOLK.

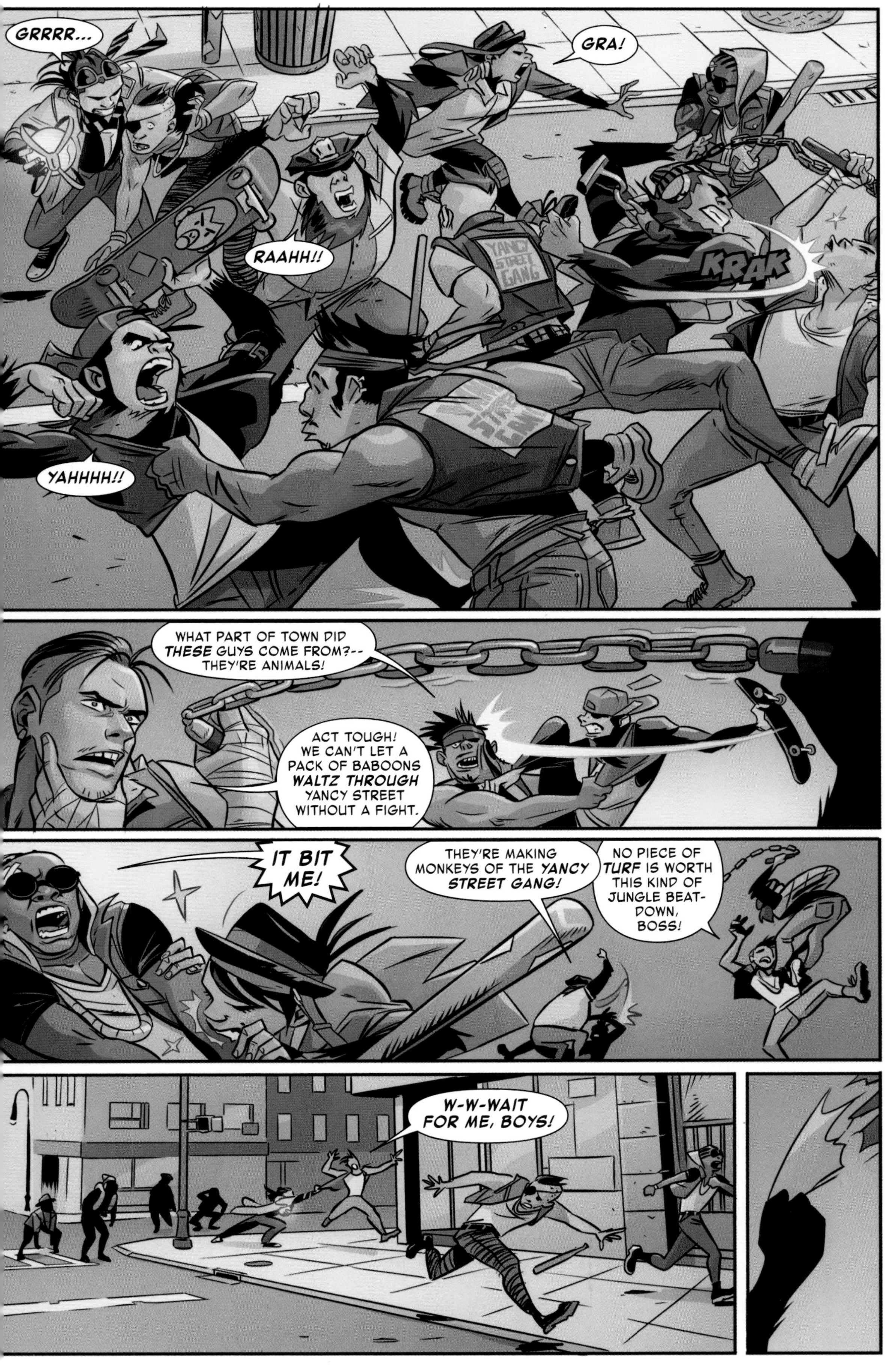
GRRRR...
GRA!
RAAHH!!
YANCY STREET GANG
KRAK
YAHHHH!!
WHAT PART OF TOWN DID THESE GUYS COME FROM?-- THEY'RE ANIMALS!
ACT TOUGH! WE CAN'T LET A PACK OF BABOONS WALTZ THROUGH YANCY STREET WITHOUT A FIGHT.
IT BIT ME!
THEY'RE MAKING MONKEYS OF THE YANCY STREET GANG!
NO PIECE OF TURF IS WORTH THIS KIND OF JUNGLE BEAT-DOWN, BOSS!
W-W-WAIT FOR ME, BOYS!

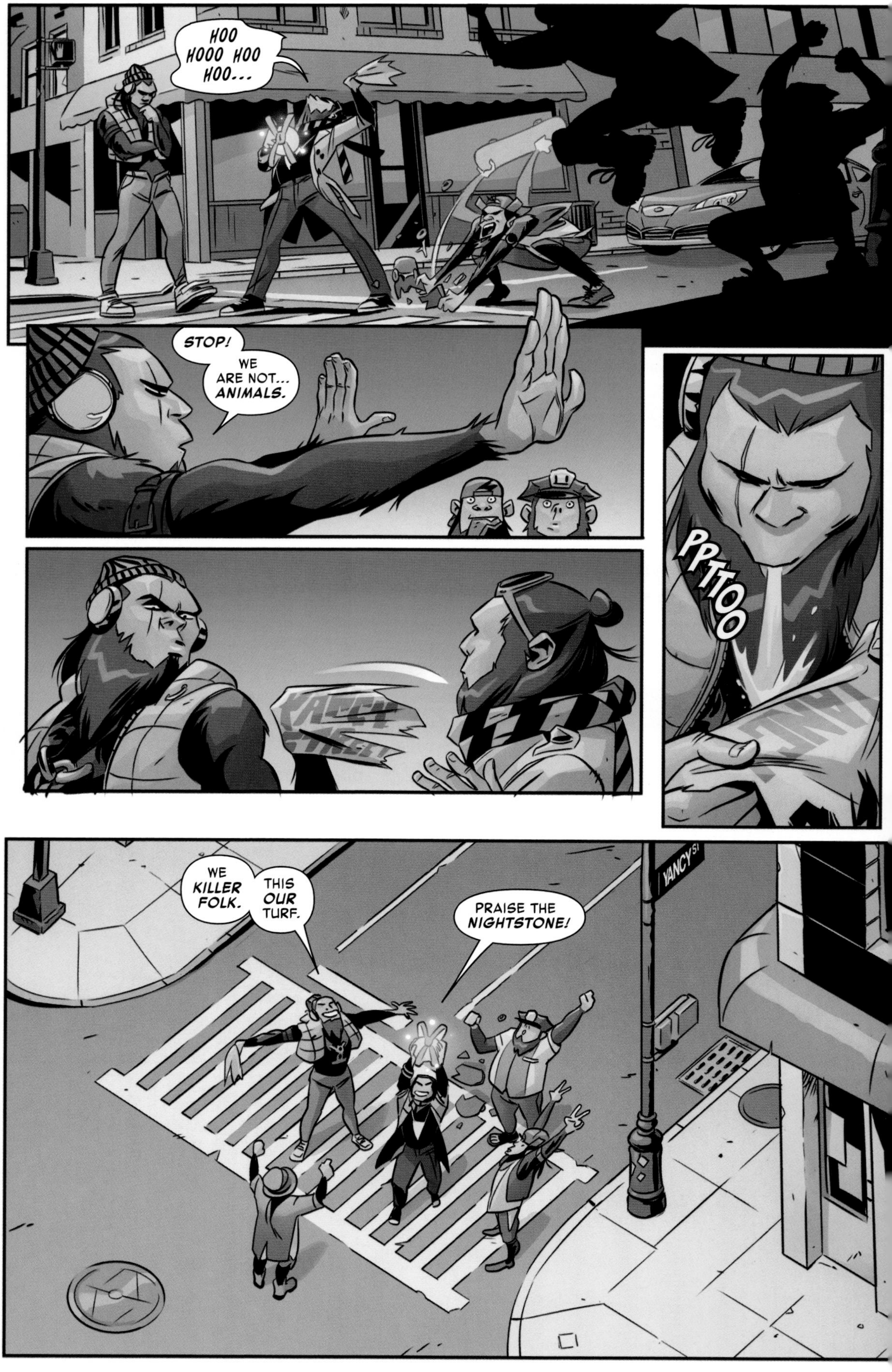
HOO HOOO HOO HOO...
STOP! WE ARE NOT... ANIMALS.
PPTTOO
WE KILLER FOLK.
THIS OUR TURF.
PRAISE THE NIGHTSTONE!
YANCY ST

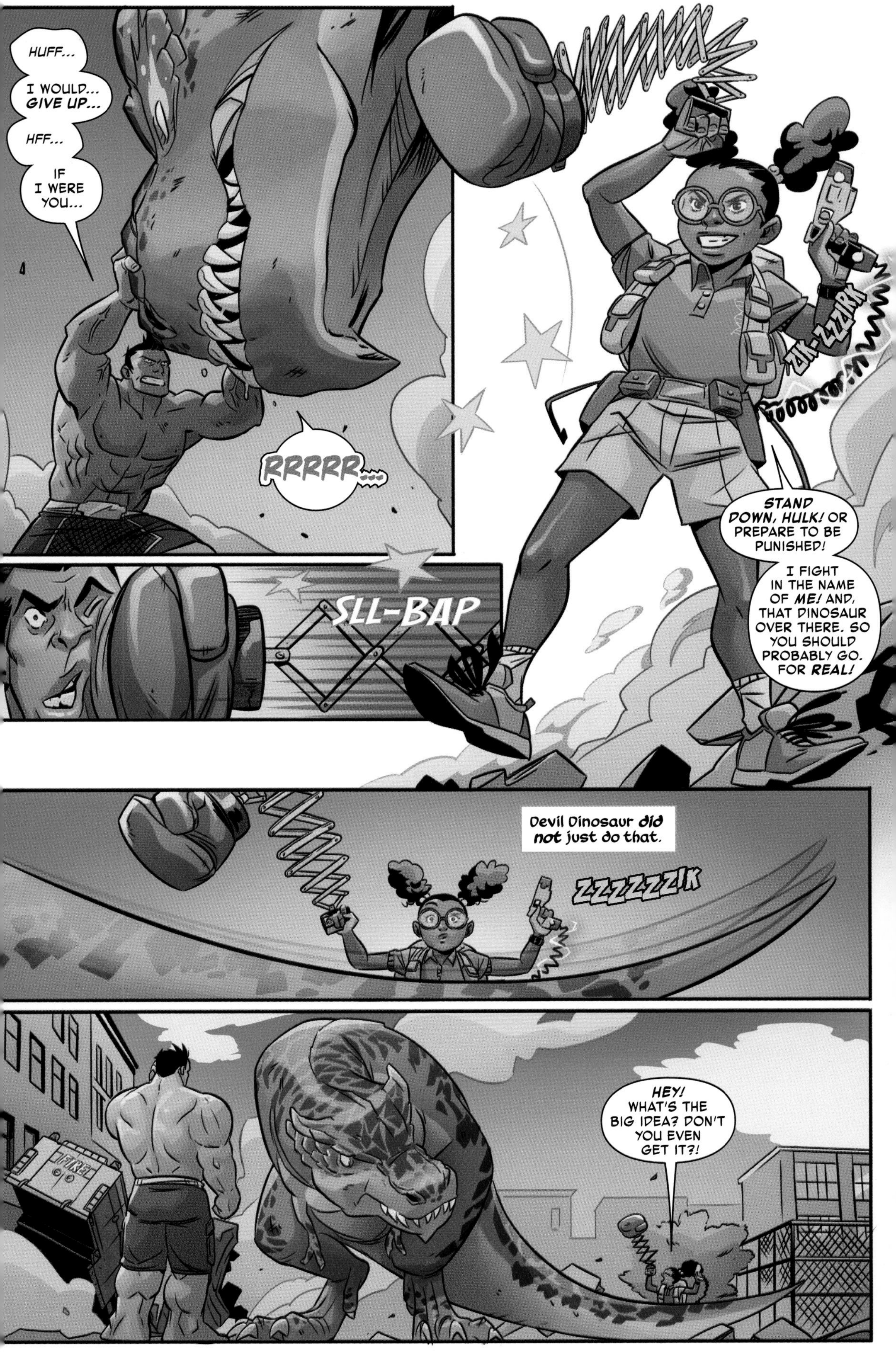
HUFF...
I WOULD... GIVE UP...
HFF...
IF I WERE YOU...
RRRRR...
STAND DOWN, HULK! OR PREPARE TO BE PUNISHED!
I FIGHT IN THE NAME OF ME! AND, THAT DINOSAUR OVER THERE. SO YOU SHOULD PROBABLY GO. FOR REAL!
ZIK-ZZZIRK
SLL-BAP
Devil Dinosaur did not just do that.
ZZZZZZIK
HEY! WHAT'S THE BIG IDEA? DON'T YOU EVEN GET IT?!
FIRE

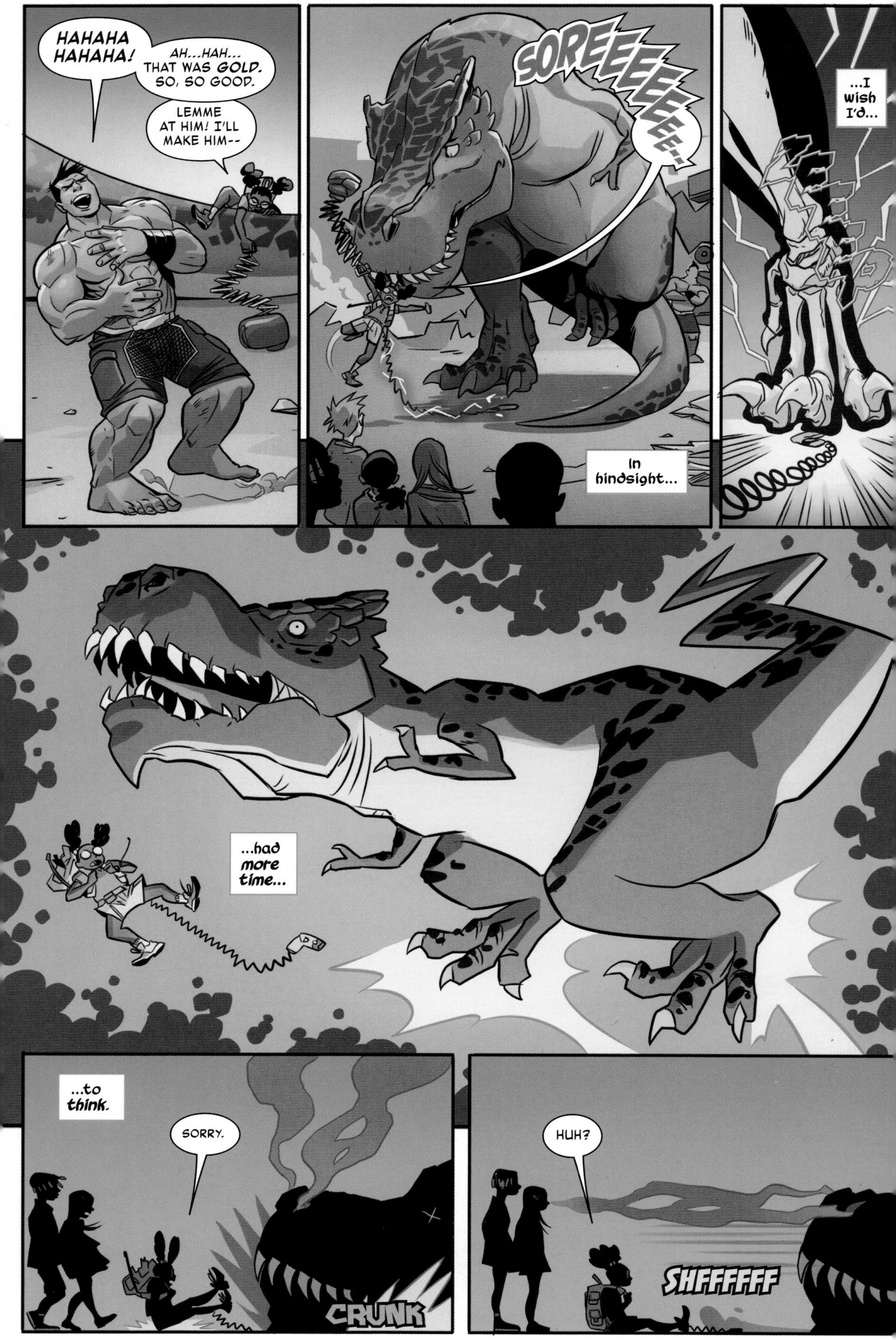

HAHAHA HAHAHA!
AH...HAH... THAT WAS GOLD. SO, SO GOOD.
LEMME AT HIM! I'LL MAKE HIM--
SOREEEEEEE..!
In hindsight...
...I wish I'd...
...had more time...
...to think.
SORRY.
CRUNK
HUH?
SHFFFFFF

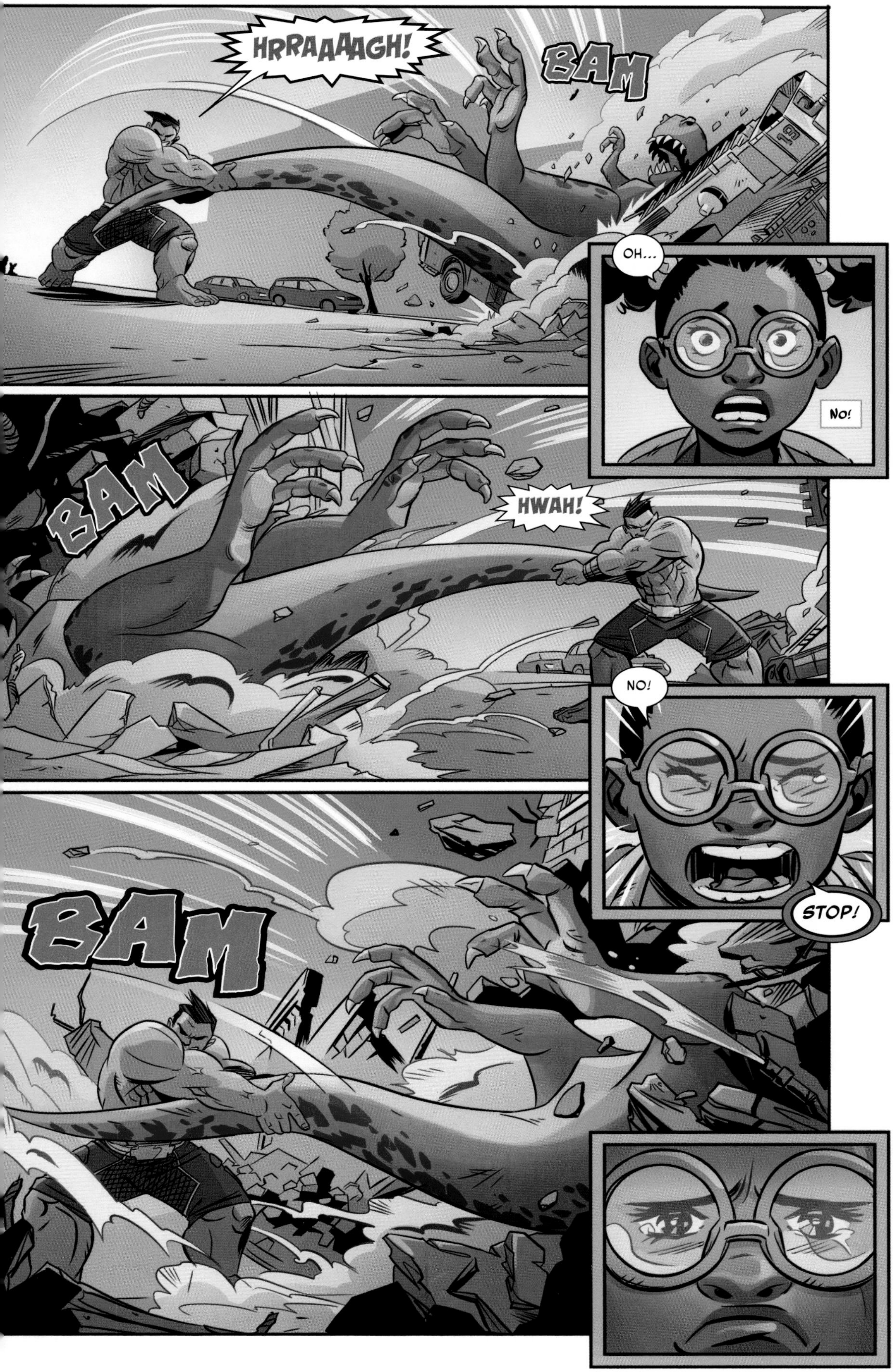
HRRAAAAGH!
BAM
OH...
NO!
BAM
HWAH!
NO!
STOP!
BAM

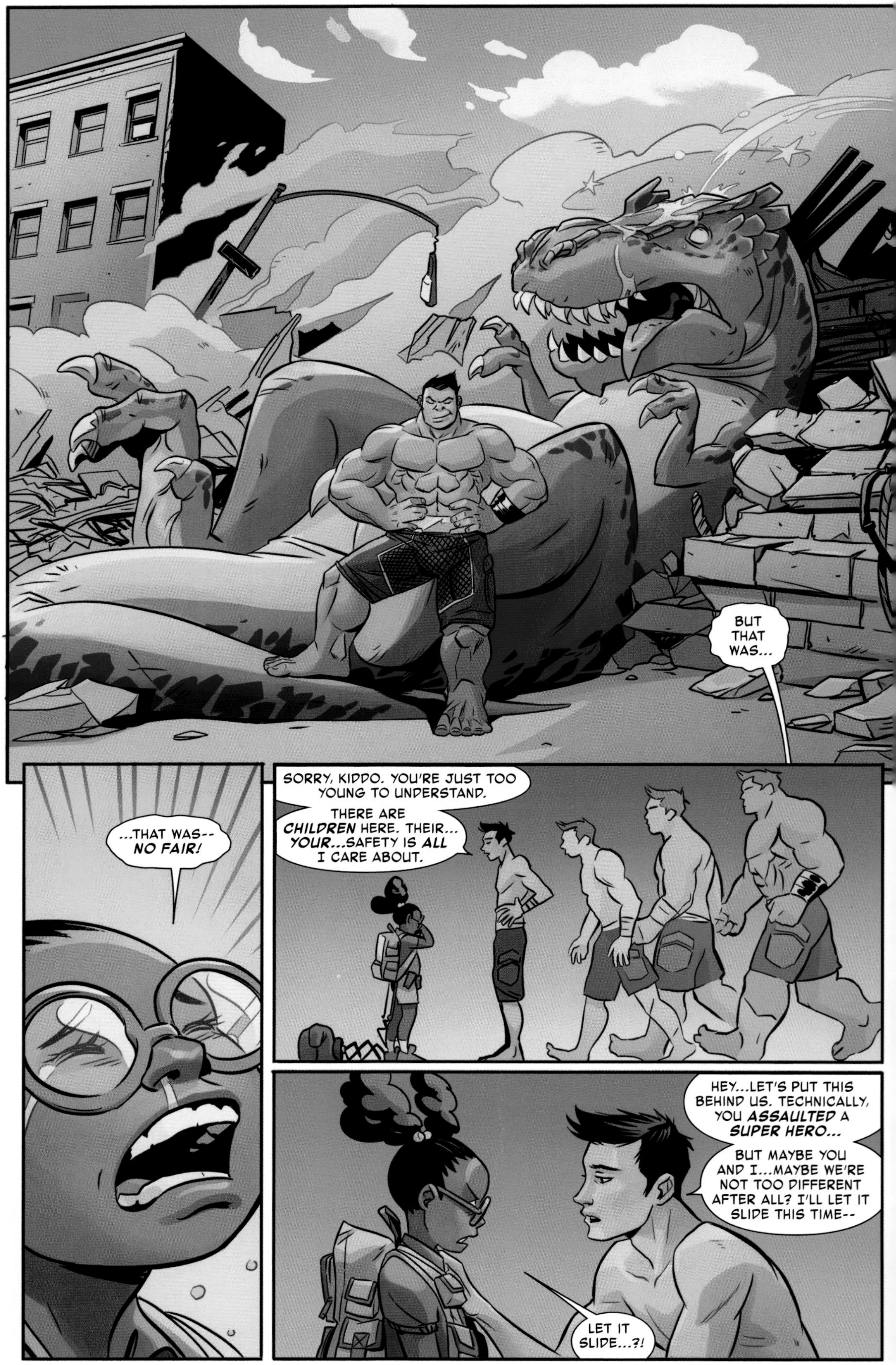
BUT THAT WAS...
...THAT WAS-- NO FAIR!
SORRY, KIDDO. YOU'RE JUST TOO YOUNG TO UNDERSTAND.
THERE ARE CHILDREN HERE. THEIR... YOUR...SAFETY IS ALL I CARE ABOUT.
HEY...LET'S PUT THIS BEHIND US. TECHNICALLY, YOU ASSAULTED A SUPER HERO...
BUT MAYBE YOU AND I...MAYBE WE'RE NOT TOO DIFFERENT AFTER ALL? I'LL LET IT SLIDE THIS TIME--
LET IT SLIDE...?!

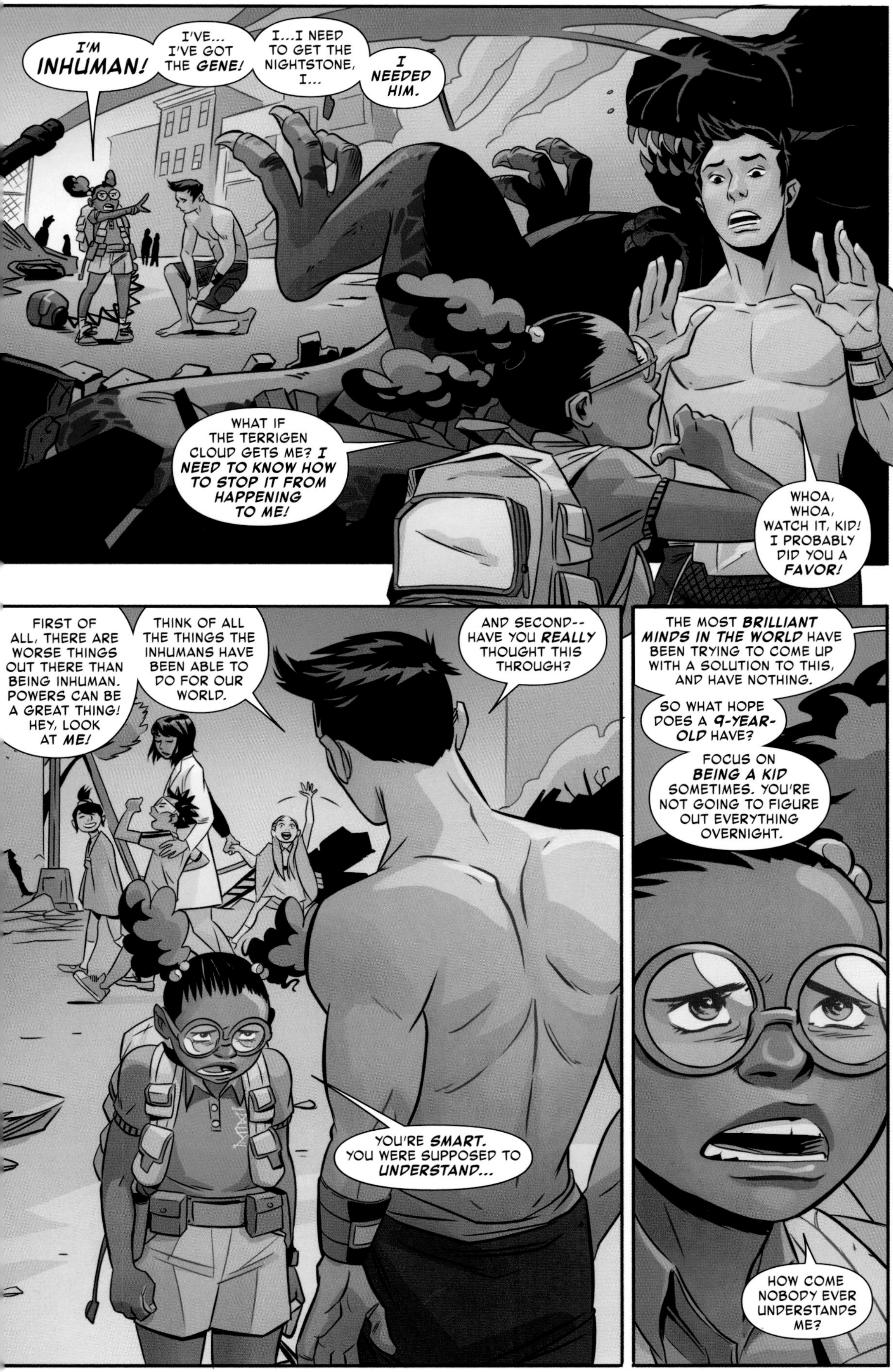
I'M INHUMAN!
I'VE... I'VE GOT THE GENE!
I...I NEED TO GET THE NIGHTSTONE, I...
I NEEDED HIM.
WHAT IF THE TERRIGEN CLOUD GETS ME? I NEED TO KNOW HOW TO STOP IT FROM HAPPENING TO ME!
WHOA, WHOA, WATCH IT, KID! I PROBABLY DID YOU A FAVOR!
FIRST OF ALL, THERE ARE WORSE THINGS OUT THERE THAN BEING INHUMAN. POWERS CAN BE A GREAT THING! HEY, LOOK AT ME!
THINK OF ALL THE THINGS THE INHUMANS HAVE BEEN ABLE TO DO FOR OUR WORLD.
AND SECOND-- HAVE YOU REALLY THOUGHT THIS THROUGH?
YOU'RE SMART. YOU WERE SUPPOSED TO UNDERSTAND...
THE MOST BRILLIANT MINDS IN THE WORLD HAVE BEEN TRYING TO COME UP WITH A SOLUTION TO THIS, AND HAVE NOTHING.
SO WHAT HOPE DOES A 9-YEAR-OLD HAVE?
FOCUS ON BEING A KID SOMETIMES. YOU'RE NOT GOING TO FIGURE OUT EVERYTHING OVERNIGHT.
HOW COME NOBODY EVER UNDERSTANDS ME?

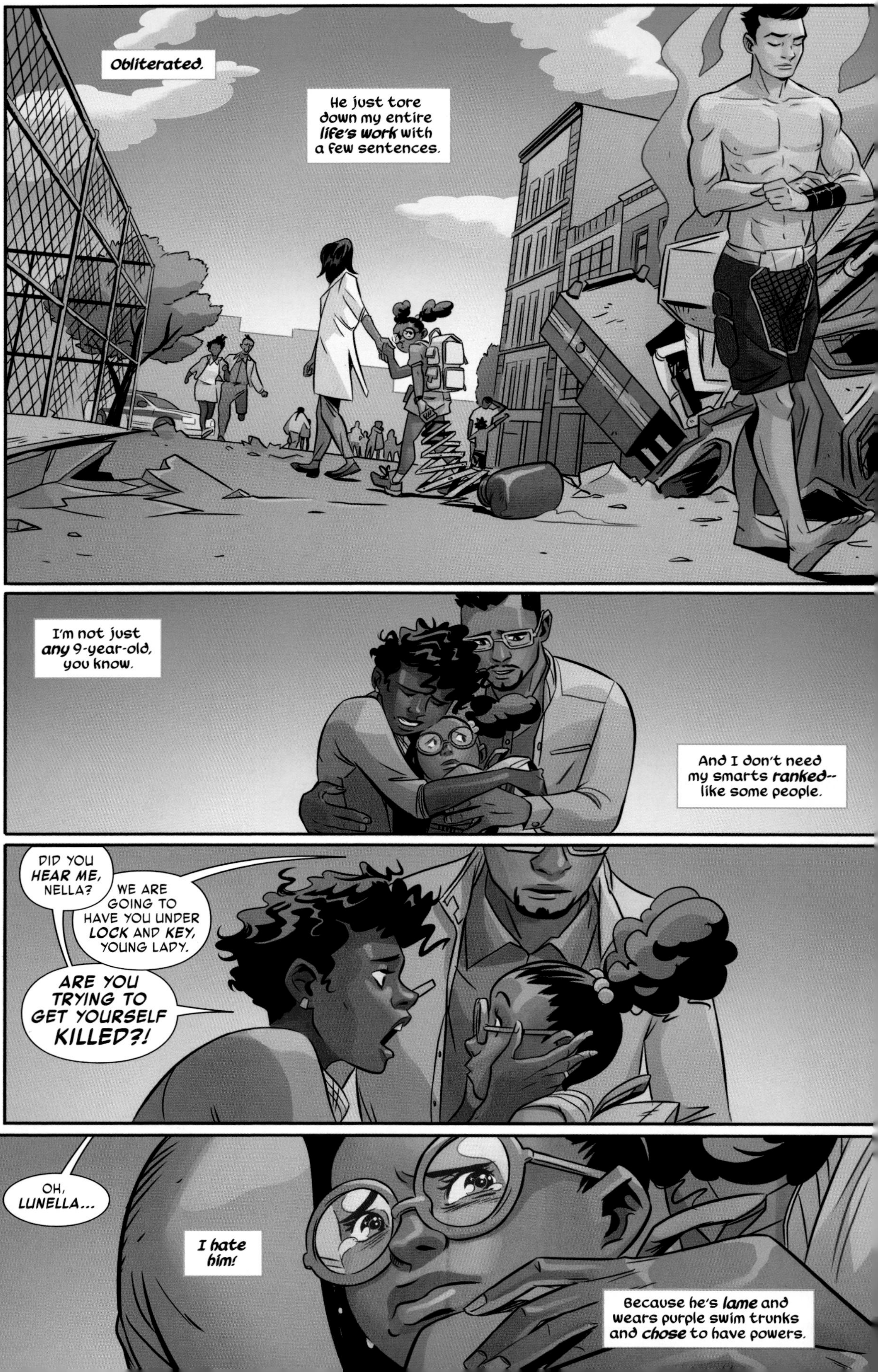
Obliterated.
He just tore down my entire *life's work* with a few sentences.
I'm not just *any* 9-year-old, you know.
And I don't need my smarts *ranked*-- like some people.
DID YOU *HEAR ME,* NELLA?
WE ARE GOING TO HAVE YOU UNDER *LOCK* AND *KEY,* YOUNG LADY.
ARE YOU TRYING TO GET YOURSELF KILLED?!
OH, *LUNELLA...*
I hate him!
Because he's *lame* and wears purple swim trunks and *chose* to have powers.

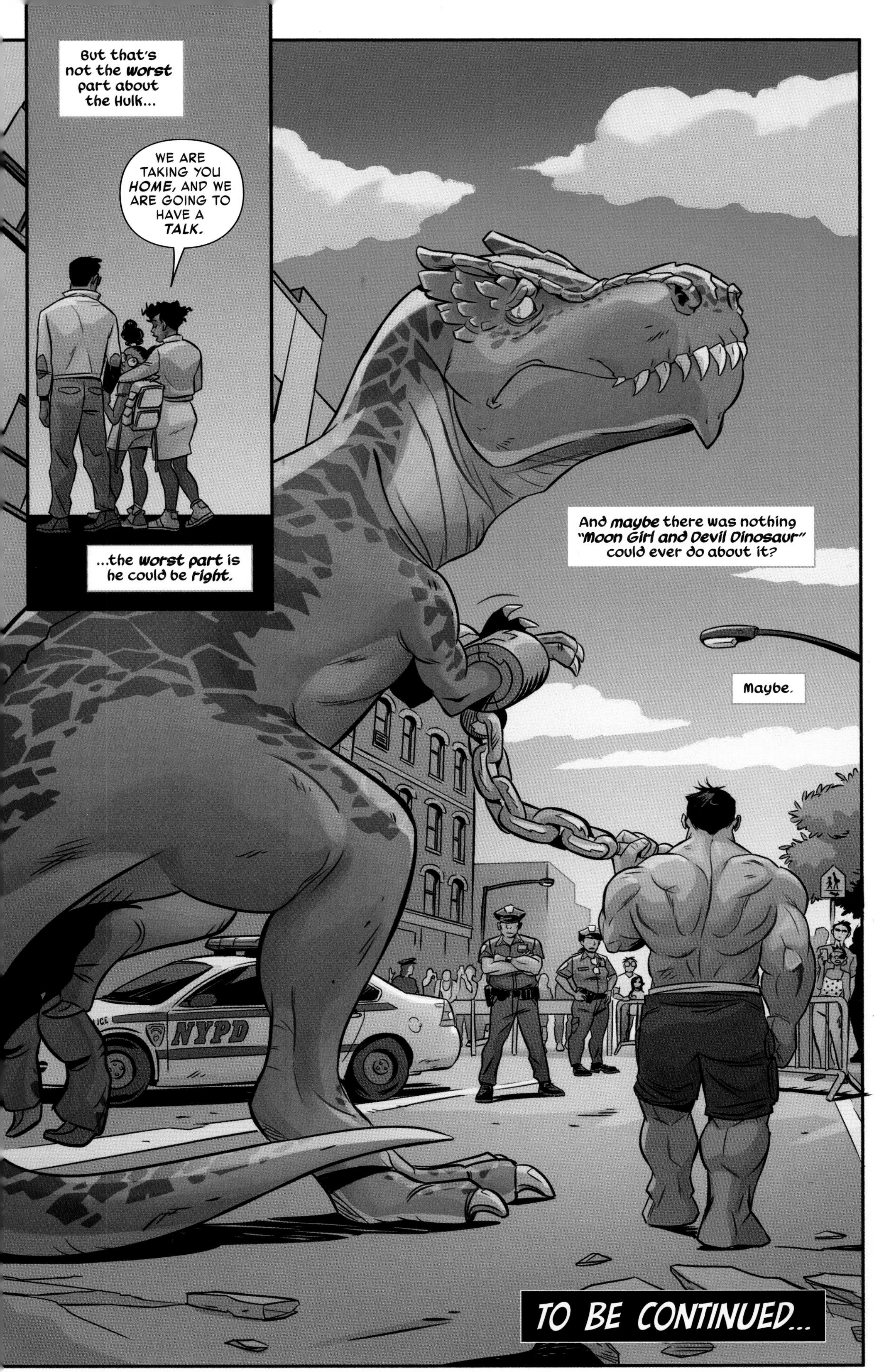
But that's not the *worst* part about the Hulk...
WE ARE TAKING YOU *HOME*, AND WE ARE GOING TO HAVE A *TALK*.
...the *worst part* is he could be *right*.
And *maybe* there was nothing *"Moon Girl and Devil Dinosaur"* could ever do about it?
Maybe.
NYPD
TO BE CONTINUED...

MOON GIRL AND DEVIL DINOSAUR™

COLLECT THEM ALL!

Set of 6 Hardcover Books ISBN: 978-1-5321-4007-5

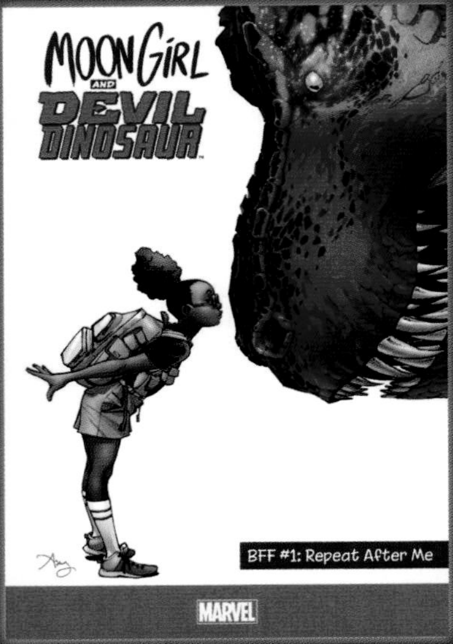
MOON GIRL AND DEVIL DINOSAUR
BFF #1: Repeat After Me
MARVEL

Hardcover Book ISBN 978-1-5321-4008-2

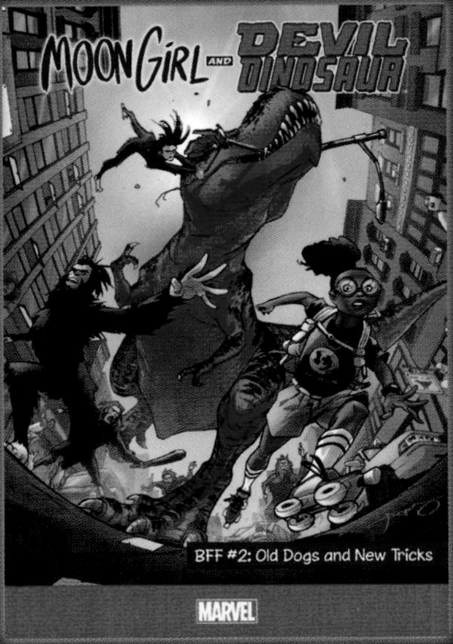
MOON GIRL AND DEVIL DINOSAUR
BFF #2: Old Dogs and New Tricks
MARVEL

Hardcover Book ISBN 978-1-5321-4009-9

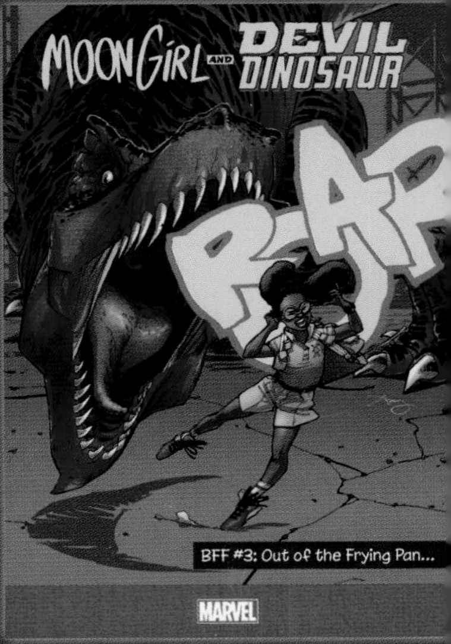
MOON GIRL AND DEVIL DINOSAUR
BFF #3: Out of the Frying Pan...
MARVEL

Hardcover Book ISBN 978-1-5321-4010-5

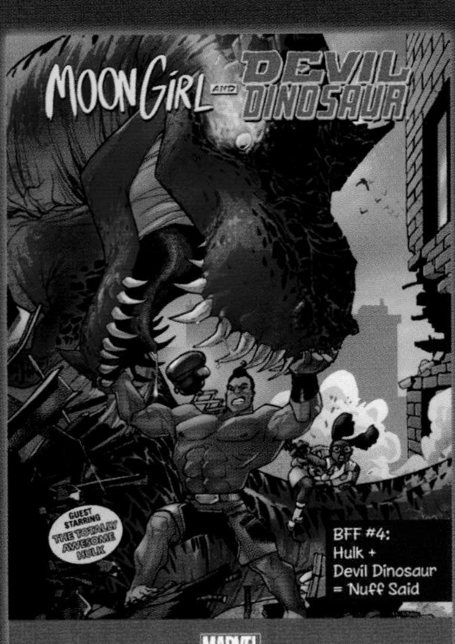
MOON GIRL AND DEVIL DINOSAUR
GUEST STARRING THE TOTALLY AWESOME HULK
BFF #4: Hulk + Devil Dinosaur = Nuff Said
MARVEL

Hardcover Book ISBN 978-1-5321-4011-2

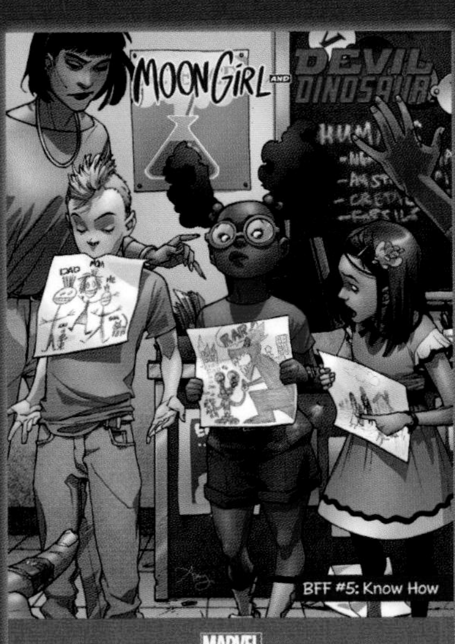
MOON GIRL AND DEVIL DINOSAUR
BFF #5: Know How
MARVEL

Hardcover Book ISBN 978-1-5321-4012-9

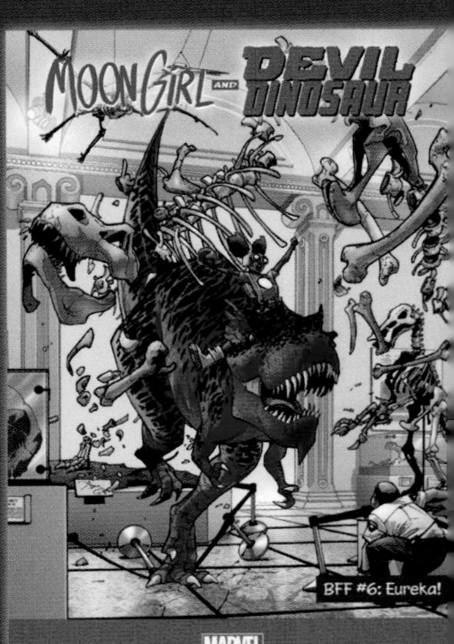
MOON GIRL AND DEVIL DINOSAUR
BFF #6: Eureka!
MARVEL

Hardcover Book ISBN 978-1-5321-4013-6